GEOGRA-FLEAS!

Riddles All over the Map

Joan Holub

Illustrated by Regan Dunnick

For George Hallowell, who loves to travel.—J.H.
To my family, and most of all, Stretch.—R.D.

Library of Congress Cataloging-in-Publication Data

Holub, Joan.
Geogra-fleas! : riddles all over the map / by Joan Holub ; illustrated by Regan Dunnick.
p. cm.
ISBN 0-8075-2818-8
1. Riddles. 2. Geography—Miscellanea. I. Title.
PN6371.H54 2004 398.6—dc22 2004000525

Published in 2004 by Albert Whitman & Company, 6340 Oakton Street, Morton Grove, Illinois 60053-2723.
Published simultaneously in Canada by Fitzhenry & Whiteside, Markham, Ontario.
Printed in the United States of America.
10 9 8 7 6 5 4 3 2 1

The paintings are rendered in watercolor and pencil on paper.
The design is by Carol Gildar.

For information about Albert Whitman & Company, please visit our web site at www.albertwhitman.com.

This little puppy
went to Paris.

This little puppy
went to Nome.

This little puppy
went to Cairo.

This little puppy
went to Rome.

This little puppy
got geogra-fleas
and scratched
the whole way home!

The Blue Planet

Name That Planet

I'm shaped like a baseball,
but you can't throw me.
I have a core,
but I'm not an apple.
I have a crust,
but I'm not toast.
I'm covered with plates,
but I'm not a table.
You step on me,
but I'm not a mat.

What am I?

Earth

Imaginary Line

I am a line of latitude—
the very longest one.
I have a belt-like attitude.
I get a lot of sun.
I divide the world in half.
I lie right in between
the hemispheres of North and South,
but I cannot be seen.

What am I?

The equator

What do you call
a puppy that runs
around the earth?

Dog-tired

Tilted

The earth is built
with a little tilt.
That's one of the reasons
we have four seasons.

What's the other reason?

The earth revolves around the sun.

Puppy and Pig

"Good day," said Patrick Puppy
when he phoned his pal Pete Pig.
Pete squealed back at Patrick,
"Have you flipped your puppy wig?
It's twelve o'clock. I was in bed.
It's dark for goodness sake."
"No way! It's day," said Patrick.
"And I am wide awake."

Why is Pete Pig asleep at twelve midnight while Patrick Puppy is wide awake?

The earth rotates on its axis every twenty-four hours. So only half of the earth is lit by the sun at any one time. Pete Pig lives in China where it is midnight. Patrick Puppy lives in South Carolina where it's noon.

The Biggest Ocean

The number of oceans
on Earth is four.
I am the biggest
from shore to shore.
I'm 64 million
square miles or more.
It's 2.67 miles
down to my floor.
I bathe California,
Japan, Ecuador,
and was named by Magellan,
who came to explore.

Which ocean am I?

The Pacific Ocean

As oceans go,
this one's gigantic.
It's twice as big
as the Atlantic.

Second Biggest Ocean

Columbus sailed across me
with three ships and a crew.
America is what he found,
in 1492.

Which ocean am I?

The Atlantic Ocean

abulous Oceans

At the North Pole

I'm on top of the world.
Isn't that nice?
I'm frozen ocean.
Not land; just ice.

Which ocean am I?

The Arctic Ocean
(The smallest and coldest ocean)

Wet and Warm

I'm the warmest ocean,
which makes me unique.
I stretch from Australia
west to Mozambique.

Which ocean am I?

The Indian Ocean

Water covers
3/4 of the
earth's surface.

How does a puppy row a boat?

With dog paddles

Cool Continents

Vacation Destination

Tourists travel hours to see
the famous art in Italy.
Tourists often are quite smitten
with the castles in Great Britain.
Tourists come by car and plane
to visit Norway, France, and Spain.
Tourists come by ship and train
to visit Greece and see Ukraine.
Tourists by the bunch vacation
at this old world destination.

Which continent is this?

Europe

What do dogs carry their
belongings in when they travel?

Doggie bags

Size: Big

I have the biggest country.
I have the Dead-est Sea.
Three-fifths of Earth's people
live on top of me.
I touch three of the oceans,
but my true claim to fame
is I'm the biggest continent.
Do you know my name?

Asia

Top to Bottom

Greenland and Canada
are the farthest north I go.
My middle is the U.S.A.
And next comes Mexico.
Smaller countries dot the land
that stretches out below.
Then I touch South America
with my tippy toe.

Which continent am I?

North America

Old and New

The Incas built an empire here,
but it's been gone 500 years.
Sir Frances Drake once sailed his ship
around Cape Horn at my south tip.
The Amazon Rainforest in Brazil
grew long ago and grows here still.

Which continent am I?

South America

At the South Pole

At the bottom of the world
lies the chilly South Pole,
in the middle of a land
penguin colonies patrol.
The stratosphere above it
has an ozone hole,
which atmospheric scientists
are trying to control.

Which continent is this?

Antarctica

G'day Mate!

Toss another shrimp
on the barbie-cue!
Hop to the outback
like a kangaroo.
It's south of the equator,
so is it any wonder
this continent's called
the "land down under"?

Which continent is this?

Australia

You'll Spot a Lot of Lions

I've got a lot of desert,
so I've got a lot of sand.
I've got a lot of countries,
and I've got a lot of land.
I've got a lot of pyramids;
a lot of jungles, too.
I've got a lot of lions,
and they aren't kept in a zoo!

Which continent am I?

Africa

More Cool Continents

What's a name for a puppy
that lives in a desert
in Africa?

A hot dog

Not Fancy

A farmer's crops will easily grow
on this flat land that's rich and low.
But since it would be hard to hide
on this grassland that stretches wide
with scattered trees and not one peak—
this land's no place for hide-and-seek.

What is it?

A plain or savannah

What's a dog's
favorite game?

Dog tag

Land Formations

Moving Hills

What kind of hills
can change and shift
when strong winds cause
their sands to drift?

Sand dunes

A Dry Heat

It's not a beach.
It's hot, dry land.
Except for oases,
it's mostly sand.

What is it?

A desert

Tall

I have a ridge or peak.
I vertically soar.
I rise from my surroundings
1,000 feet or more.

What am I?

A mountain

Flat Top

It's steep like a mountain,
but flat on top like a plate.
(It's formed when upward thrust
makes the earth's crust elevate.)

What is it?

A plateau

Almost an Island

It's land that sticks out far
into oceans, lakes, or seas.
With water on three sides,
Florida's one of these.

What is it?

A peninsula

Shorter

I'm smaller than a mountain
and may have a rounded top.
Somewhere below 1,000 feet
is where I usually stop.

What am I?

A hill

Around-the-World Super Sizes

The Biggest Desert

How dry I am.
How dry I'll be,
since little rain
falls down on me.
Umbrellas aren't
seen much around
North Africa,
where I am found.

What am I?

The Sahara Desert
(more than 3,500,000 square miles)

What do you call a
puppy that climbs
up to a peak?

Top dog

The Tallest Peak

I'm famous 'round the world
for my elevation.
Asia's Himalayas
are my mountainous location.
People love to climb me,
and here's the reason why—
I'm 29, 035 feet high!

What am I?

Mount Everest

The Longest River

From my waters Tut once drank.
Nefertiti sat on my riverbank.
Cleopatra sipped from me
as I flowed north to the Mediterranean Sea.
(But today it's just the silent sphinx
that remembers all those ancient drinks.)

What am I?

The Nile River
(4,160 miles long)

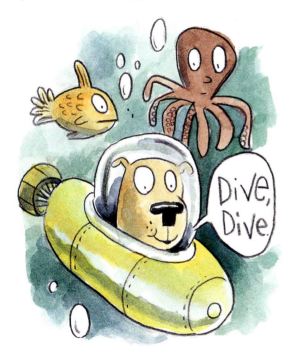

Deepest Point under Water

I'm a place in the ocean
that's down, down deep
where it's gloomy, mysterious,
still, and asleep.

What am I?

Challenger Deep, Mariana Trench,
Pacific Ocean
(35,840 feet deep)

The Largest Island

I'm mostly ice-covered and white,
so my name doesn't fit me quite right.
My big icebergs caused a panic
when they sank the ship *Titanic*
in the Northern Atlantic one night.

What am I?

Greenland
(836,330 square miles)

Guess That Country!

Tour Beijing's Forbidden City.
Have dim sum, chow mein, and tea.
See the Temple of Confucius
built in 478 B.C.
Walk along the Great Wall
that once kept the Mongols out.
Hear Mandarin and Cantonese
both spoken on your route.

China

Ride a camel through the desert
till you reach the river Nile.
Shop outdoor bazaars in Cairo.
Try to get a sphinx to smile.
Walk through the Valley of the Kings.
See Giza's pyramids.
View King Tut's ancient mummy,
and its golden coffin lids.

Egypt

What kind of eating utensils
will a dog fetch?

Chopsticks

Where do dogs shop?

At flea markets

Read the Roman numerals
carved into the Colosseum.
See a Botticelli painting
in a Vatican museum.
Ride a gondola in Venice.
Have a yummy pizza pie.
See the Leaning Tower of Pisa.
Now say "ciao," which means "good-bye."

Italy

Hear mariachi music
in a tall beachside hotel.
Surf waves at Acapulco.
Scuba dive at Cozumel.
Meet dancers in sombreros.
See masks made by Aztecs.
Tour stony ancient ruins
built by Mayan architects.

Mexico

Climb the Eiffel Tower.
Eat a toasty warm baguette.
Watch Parisian ballet dancers
as they twirl and pirouette.
Take a look around the Louvre
to see great works of art.
Learn about an emperor
whose name was Bonaparte.

France

What's a dog's favorite painting
in the Louvre museum in Paris?

The Bone-a Lisa!

Hooray for the U.S.A.!

Great States

The United States of America
was once land undivided.
Its first state was Delaware.
(I wonder who decided?)
More states joined, one by one,
to stand in strength beside it.
Hawaii was the last of all.
(I'm glad it was invited.)
How many states are there now
in this land, united?

Fifty

Name the U.S.A.'s Neighbors:

South is a country that starts with **M**.
North is a country that starts with **C**.
East is an ocean that starts with **A**.
West is an ocean that starts with **P**.

Answers:
South: Mexico
North: Canada
East: Atlantic Ocean
West: Pacific Ocean

If Dogs Ran the U.S.A. . . . .

What would the national bird be?

A beagle eagle

Where would the presidential puppy live?

The White Dog House

Which dog would be the most patriotic?

A yankee doodle poodle

What kind of geography books
would everyone read?

Dog-eared ones

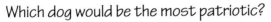

What would the nickname for the country be?

Dalmation Nation

How would the pioneers
have traveled west?

By tail-waggin' train

What famous document would
Thomas Jefferson have helped write?

The Doglaration of Independence

What would the two major
political parties be?

Dog-macrats and Flea-publicans

We're All Wet

There are five of us.
Our pools connect.
In our fresh waters,
ships have wrecked.
We touch Canada
and eight states, too.
We're smaller than the oceans,
but every bit as blue.

What are we?

The Great Lakes
(Erie, Huron, Michigan,
Ontario, Superior)

Gorge-ous

The Colorado River
eroded the land
in Arizona state
and carved something grand.
The Colorado River
roared along its way
to dig this giant chasm
that remains today.

What is it?

The Grand Canyon

Landmarks

Slightly Batty

Passageways.
Underground.
Cold, dark halls.
Spooky sound.
Stalactites
dripping down.
Bats hanging
all around.
In Kentucky,
I'm found.

What am I?

Mammoth Caves

Mighty

I'm mighty long.
I'm mighty strong.
I'm sailed by barges and ships.
From Minnesota I flow
to the Gulf of Mexico
on countless river trips.

What am I?

The Mississippi River

U.S.A. Big and Small

R.I.

The Biggest State

I am the 49th state.
My capital is Juneau.
I'm famous for a dog-sled race,
oil, Inuit, bears, and snow.
You'll find tall Mt. McKinley
in my Denali Park.
Come visit me in summer
when it's hardly ever dark.

What state am I?

Alaska
(615,230 square miles—
more than twice as big as
Texas, the second-largest state.)

The Smallest State

I'm very small, and that's why
mapmakers draw me and sigh.
There's no room for my name.
So although it's a shame,
on maps I get labeled R.I.

What state am I?

Rhode Island
(1,231 square miles)

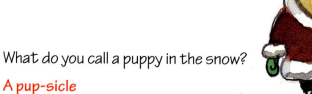

What do you call a puppy in the snow?

A pup-sicle

U.S.A. Amazing Facts!

Brrrr

Which state is the farthest north
of all 50 states in the U.S.A.?

Alaska
(Ask your friends and see if
they guess Maine or Washington.)

Which state is the farthest south
of all 50 states in the U.S.A.?

Hawaii
(Ask your friends and see if
they guess Texas or Florida.)

Which state is the farthest west
of all 50 states in the U.S.A.?

Alaska
(Ask your friends and see if
they guess California or Hawaii.)

Which state is the farthest east
of all 50 states in the U.S.A.?

Alaska
(Surprising, but true!
Alaska's Aleutian Island chain passes the 180th meridian,
which is the global dividing line between all eastern and western
longitudes. This means Alaska has the easternmost, westernmost,
and northernmost spots in the U. S. A.!)

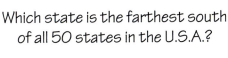

State Picture Riddles

Tennessee

Arkansas

Rhode Island

Pennsylvania

New Jersey

Idaho

Silly State Riddles

In what state do you often hear a quack?

South Duck-ota (South Dakota)

Which state sneezes a lot?

Ill-inois

Which state doesn't use bottles?

Kan-sas

Which state can stay warm in winter?

North Da-coat-a (North Dakota)

Which state has the most happy people?

Merry-land (Maryland)

Which state has lots of smart people?

Wise-consin (Wisconsin)

Which states wear glasses with three lenses?

**Illinois, Virginia, and West Virginia
(because each has three eyes)**

Which state has the most acorns?

Oak-lahoma (Oklahoma)

Which state has lots of gum?

Massa-chew-setts (Massachusetts)

In which state do people do a ton of laundry?

In Washing-ton

In Which State Can You . . .

Visit a volcano.
Wear a fragrant orchid lei.
Spend time at Pearl Harbor's
ship memorial display.
Climb a tree for coconuts.
Enjoy exotic plants.
Eat poi at a luau.
Do a swaying hula dance.

Hawaii

Watch the oil rigs pumping
in the Gulf of Mexico.
Yee-haw! Meet some cowboys
riding in a rodeo.
Visit Dallas, Austin, Houston.
Don't miss San Antonio,
where the famous Davy Crockett
once fought at the Alamo.

Texas

See the Smoky Mountains.
Hear the hills of Nashville ring
with country western music
Grand Ole Opry crooners sing.
Boogie down in Memphis,
like a rockabilly fan.
And hail the king of rock 'n roll.
That's Elvis Presley, man!

Tennessee

Did you hear about the dog
singing contest?

It was a howl.

See Cape Canaveral's rockets.
Try to catch sight of mermaids
as you watch for alligators
swimming in the Everglades.
Beachcomb on Miami's shores
beneath the tall palm trees.
Search for shipwrecked treasure
in small islands called the Keys.

Florida

Hurry to New Orleans
for the Mardi Gras parades.
Eat some jambalaya.
Hear jazz trumpet serenades.
Sail the Mississippi.
Find a bayou to explore.
View a big plantation
built before the Civil War.

Louisiana

Tour Sutter's Mill where gold
was found in 1848.
Cross a San Francisco bridge
that's called the Golden Gate.
Gaze at stars in Hollywood.
Thrill ride at Disneyland.
Watch the waves come crashing down
on white Pacific sand.

California

What kind of dogs joined the gold rush?

Gold-en retrievers

State Capital Picture Riddles

Boise
(Idaho)

Jackson
(Mississippi)

Topeka
(Kansas)

Little Rock
(Arkansas)

Columbia
(South Carolina)

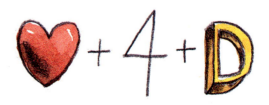

Hartford
(Connecticut)

Kooky State Capital Riddles

Which capital city sells things at a discount?

Sale-m (Salem, Oregon)

Which capital city is wealthy?

Rich-mond (Richmond, Virginia)

Which capital city likes to be in charge?

Boss-ton (Boston, Massachusetts)

Which capital city sounds like a name
for a bashful girl?

Shy Ann (Cheyenne, Wyoming)

Which capital city has only one season?

Spring-field (Springfield, Illinois)

Which capital city has only one month?

June-o (Juneau, Alaska)

Which capital city has lots of bags?

Sack-ramento (Sacramento, California)

Capital or Capitol?

Capital has an **a**.
It's a city, like Santa Fe,
capital of New Mexico,
or a place like Washington, D.C.,
capital of the U.S.A.
Okay?

Capitol has an **o**.
It's a building,
and some come
with a dome,
which is round on top
sort of like an "o,"
ya know?

Map Rap

Flower Power

It's good to know direction
when going on a quest.
My arrows point the way to go
due north, south, east, and west.

What am I?

A compass rose

Which Way?

North of me stands a dragon;
south, a slimy beast.
West is a monster with three hea[ds].
I think that I'll go __?__.

East

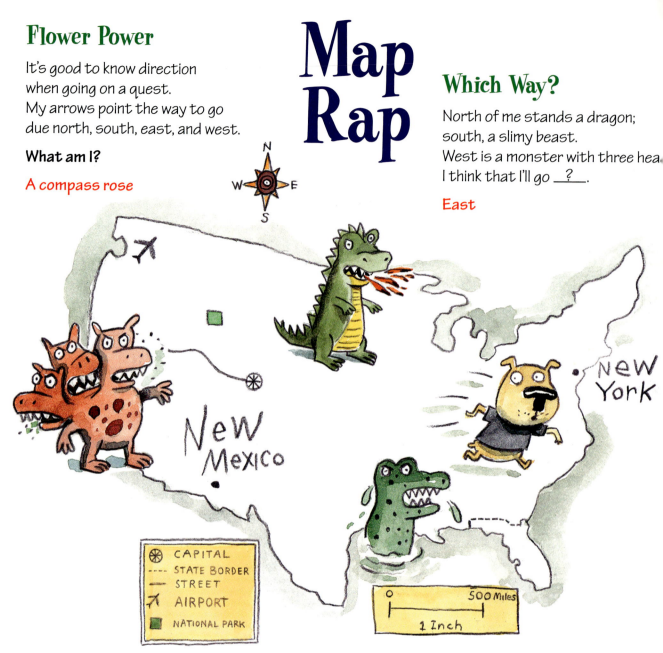

Unlock the Symbols

What is an airplane?
Or a box colored green?
I unlock maps' symbols,
so you'll know what they mean.

What am I?

A key or legend

How Far?

How many miles equal an inch?
I make measurements on maps a cinch.
(So how many miles would you have to go
from New York State to New Mexico?)

What am I?

A scale (Hint: An inch equals 500 miles.
It's 4 inches from New York to New Mexico
on the map.) So how many miles is it?
500 x 4 = 2000 miles.

A Me-Map

I've made a map as you can see.
I've made a map, and it's of me!
Up north's my wet nose and my mouth.
My waggly tail is way down south.
East is a white paw with brown spots.
West is a black paw with white dots.
I've mapped myself and shown you how.
So you can draw a you-map now!

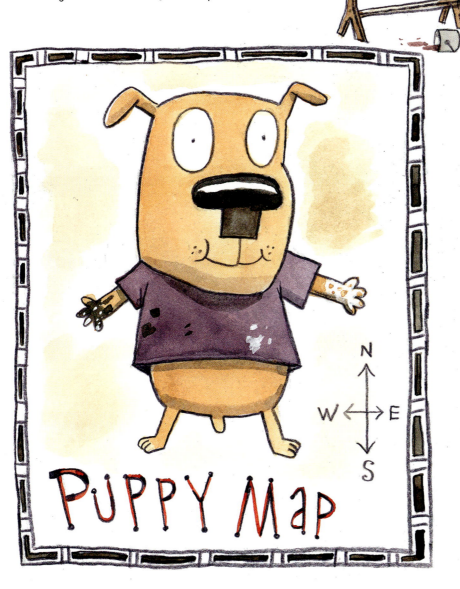

Puppy Planet Pals

Last week I met a dog in space
and gave him my address.
I invited him to Earth
to be my welcome guest.

A galaxy called Milky Way
is where you'll visit me.
I'm in the Solar System.
Earth is planet number three.
I'm on the continent—North America,
in the country—U.S.A.,
in the state of California,
and the city of L.A.,
on Barker Street inside a house
that's numbered 101.
I hope that you will visit me.
Bow-WOW! That would be fun!

(But if you visit,
 please, please, please
do <u>not</u> bring geogra-fleas!)

What do you call the last page of this book?

The tail end.